Nelly's Garden

by

❧ ELIZABETH SLOTE ❧

Tambourine Books/New York

Tambourine Books, a division of William Morrow & Company, Inc.,
105 Madison Avenue, New York, New York 10016.
Printed in the United States of America. First edition.
1 3 5 7 9 10 8 6 4 2
Library of Congress Cataloging in Publication Data
Slote, Elizabeth. Nelly's garden / by Elizabeth Slote. p. cm.
Summary: Little Nelly Dragon enjoys the different flowers
each month in her garden.
ISBN 0-688-10013-9—ISBN 0-688-10014-7 (lib. bdg.)
[1. Months—Fiction. 2. Flowers—Fiction. 3. Gardens—Fiction.
4. Dragons—Fiction.] I. Title. PZ7.S636Ne 1991
[E]—dc20 90-33382 CIP AC

For
Sophia

and
Winzie

All year long, Nelly Dragon loves to play in the garden behind her house.

In January snowflakes fall
and blanket the ground.

In February, deep beneath the snow,

spring bulbs begin to sprout.

In March snowdrops
and crocuses come up.

Daffodils
and grape hyacinths
bloom in April.

Tulips, lilies-of-the-valley,
and the apple tree blossom in May.

June is roses.

July brings bee-balm,
bluebells, and bugs.

In August Nelly leaves her garden
and goes to the ocean.

When she comes back in
September the sunflowers
have grown very, very tall.

Asters and chrysanthemums
bloom last, in October.

In November the garden
is covered with leaves.

And in December Nelly's garden
has stars and lights
that twinkle good-night.